For my mom, Cheryl,
the most gentle and kind soul,
who took in the world around her
with curiosity and wonder

SIMON & SCHUSTER BOOKS FOR YOUNG READERS
An imprint of Simon & Schuster Children's Publishing Division
1230 Avenue of the Americas, New York, New York 10020
© 2024 by Annie Herzig
Book design by Laurent Linn
Simon & Schuster: Celebrating 100 Years of Publishing in 2024
For information about special discounts for bulk purchases, please contact
Simon & Schuster Special Sales at 1-866-506-1949 or business@simonandschuster.com.
The Simon & Schuster Speakers Bureau can bring authors to your live event. For more information or to book an event,
contact the Simon & Schuster Speakers Bureau at 1-866-248-3049 or visit our website at www.simonspeakers.com.
The text for this book was set in Filson Soft Regular.
The illustrations for this book were rendered using watercolor, gouache, colored pencil, graphite, and water soluble crayon.
Manufactured in China
0824 SCP

2 4 6 8 10 9 7 5 3
Names: Herzig, Annie, author, illustrator.
Title: Wonder & awe / Annie Herzig.
Other titles: Wonder and awe
Description: First edition. | New York : Simon & Schuster Books for Young Readers, 2024. | "A Paula Wiseman Book." |
Audience: Ages 4–8. | Audience: Grades 2–3. | Summary: After befriending a snowy friend, whom she names Wonder,
a young girl's sense of awe comes alive as she rediscovers the world through her new friend's eyes.
Identifiers: LCCN 2023050804 (print) | LCCN 2023050805 (ebook) | ISBN 9781665947534 (hardcover) | ISBN 9781665947541 (ebook)
Subjects: CYAC: Wonder—Fiction. | Perspective—Fiction. | Winter—Fiction. | Snowmen—Fiction. | LCGFT: Picture books.
Classification: LCC PZ7.1.H497 Wo 2024 (print) | LCC PZ7.1.H497 (ebook) | DDC [E]—dc23
LC record available at https://lccn.loc.gov/2023050804
LC ebook record available at https://lccn.loc.gov/2023050805

WONDER & AWE

Annie Herzig

A PAULA WISEMAN BOOK
SIMON & SCHUSTER BOOKS FOR YOUNG READERS
NEW YORK LONDON TORONTO SYDNEY NEW DELHI

One magical morning, I make a new friend.

She's not from around here,

so everything is new to her.

I think
I'll call
you Wonder.

She is simply full of wonder,
and it makes me wonder . . .

How did I miss this before?

I'm in awe.

More magical days follow
with my friend at my side.

And at the end of each day,
we always say:

Good night!

Sleep tight!

One afternoon, I notice Wonder starting to lose
some of her magic. I think she knows it too.
"I may have to go soon," she says.

But...
I'll miss you.

"I'll miss you, too. But let's not worry about it now. Let's just enjoy today."

Good night.

Sleep tight.

And we do.

But the next day, my friend is gone.

Mom says spring has come early.

Next winter seems so far away.

It might as well be forever.

What if I start to forget Wonder's warm smile?

Many days pass.

Many days

with no magic.

Until . . .

I open my eyes again . . .

to the wonder all around me.

There is plenty of wonder to share.

At last, one day after school,
the air feels cold and crisp.

Mom helps me bake
springerle cookies. Those
are Wonder's favorite,
and I want to be ready,
just in case. . . .

At bedtime, Mom tucks me in and kisses me on the cheek. I think of my friend again.

Momma, do you think there will be snow tomorrow?

We shall see
what we shall
see, hon.
Good night!

Sleep tight!

The next morning, the world outside is **pure magic!**

Is it really you?

It's really me...
I've missed you.

I've missed you, too.
Come on,
I have so much to
share with you.

Together, we are filled
with wonder and awe.